Through Children's Eyes:
Tales OF OLD Columbus

Carole Gerber • Marty Husted
A Project of the Columbus Historical Society

Published by the Columbus Historical Society
51 Jefferson Avenue
Columbus, OH 43215
Phone: 614/224-0822
Email: *info@columbushistory.org*

Call or write for membership information
or visit us at *www.columbushistory.org <http://www.columbushistory.org>*
Stories © 2003 by Carole Gerber • Illustrations © 2003 by Marty Husted

ISBN 0-9742573-1-1

Foreword

This is a book of historical fiction. The stories that follow are based on facts. The boys and girls telling the stories did not exist. However, what they tell you is true:

- Aunt Sarah really did have an "unexpected" son in 1803.
- The Wyandot Indians did make moccasins for a white baby.
- Reverend Jason Bull did help runaway slaves get to Canada.
- German Village was settled by families from Germany. Many of them arrived on canal boats, just like the one in the story.
- Mr. Lincoln really did visit Columbus, where he was mobbed at the statehouse.
- Many children from New York City were adopted after they arrived on trains.
- The 1913 flood was one of Ohio's worst.

Thousands of men and women who built our city were smart, brave, honest, and strong. *Through Children's Eyes* tells you about only a few of them.

Some terminology used in this book is reflective of the era, and is used for historical context only.

Table of Contents

Acknowledgements

The Columbus Historical Society is pleased to present this book to the children of Franklin County to celebrate the Franklin County and State of Ohio Bicentennials. It represents more than three years of effort; and we believe the book is first of its kind in Central Ohio.

The inspiration for this project came from the Columbus Public Schools system when it was noted that the materials used to teach local history to third graders were nearly forty years old.

Columbus Historical Society put together a project team to develop and oversee the creation of new materials. The project team included: Sherry Buk (Columbus Historical Society), Ed Lentz, (Past Finders), Cathi Nelson (Columbus Public Schools), Mike Peppe (Hadler Realty) and Doreen Uhas-Sauer (Columbus Public Schools).

The result is this children's book, and a new Teacher's Guide to Columbus History, which will be available in early 2004.

A pilot project of 15 lesson plans was released in 2002. We thank our pilot project authors: David Burkett, Wendi Hawk, and ReVonne Williams, all CPS teachers; and our pilot sponsors: The Junior League of Columbus, Learning Design Associates, Baker & Hostetetler, LLP, and IKON.

Special thanks to the creative team for *Through Children's Eyes*, Carole Gerber (author), Marty Husted (illustrator) and Jane Hoffelt (designer). This team was tremendous, and spent countless hours working with the novices at CHS on this project.

The City of Columbus was also supportive of this effort, and we thank Mayor Michael B. Coleman, City Council President Matthew Habash, Council Members Kevin Boyce, Michael C. Mentel, Maryellen O'Shaughnessy, Richard W. Sensenbrenner, Charleta B. Tavares, and Patsy Thomas, and the Franklin County Bicentennial Association and especially Linda Haley, without whom this book would not have happened. We also thank the Franklin County Commissioners, Dewey Stokes, Mary Jo Kilroy, and Arlene Shoemaker for their support during the project. In addition to the Columbus Public Schools staff listed above, we thank the Columbus School Board and Columbus Public Schools Superintendent Dr. Gene T. Harris.

A great idea comes to fruition only with community support. Printing for this project is in partnership with Grange Insurance. The Walter and Marian English Foundation funded the creative team. We express our sincere gratitude to our sponsors for their leadership and generosity.

Finally, thank you to all unnamed individuals who participated in the project.

The Columbus Historical Society

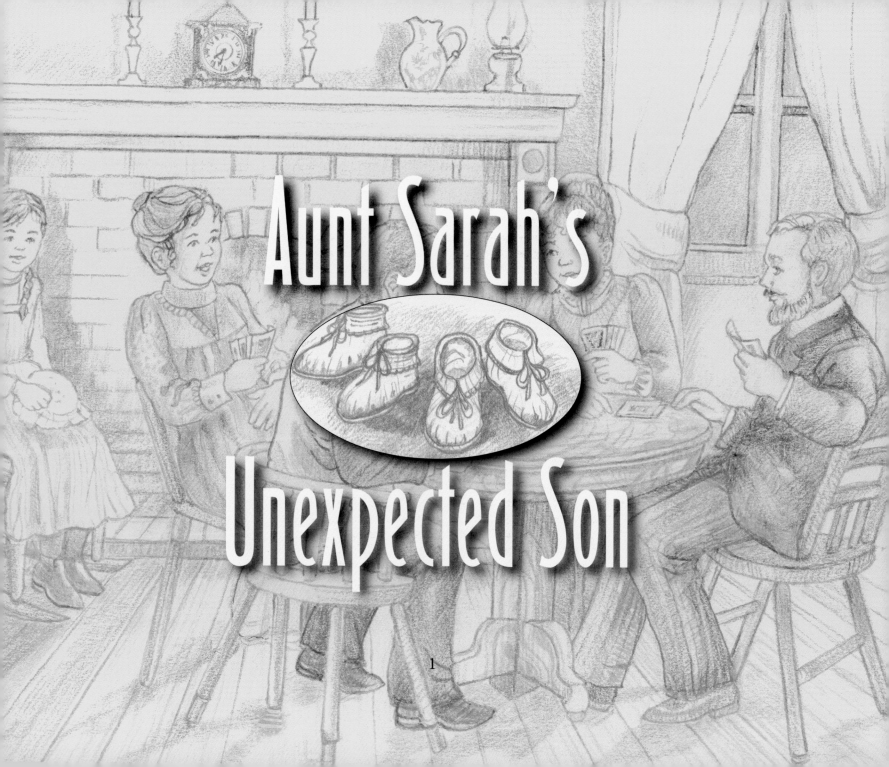

Aunt Sarah's
Unexpected Son

The four of them were hunkered around the table, playing whist. The candles flickering in the dark made the room feel as cozy as a nest. My Uncle Lucas Sullivant was dealing the cards and my Aunt Sarah was talking and giggling. She was as cheerful as a chipmunk and as round as a hen. My Ma and Pa were listening and nodding.

Ma joked that Aunt Sarah would soon hatch. "Hatch what?" I asked from the rocking chair by the fireplace. I pretended I don't know Aunt Sarah was expecting her first baby. Her cheeks turned red and she smoothed her dress over her stomach.

"Hush, Lucy!" she joked right back, pretending to slap Ma's hands. "Show some respect for your little sister who is about to win again."

Uncle Lucas didn't say much, but he smiled whenever Sarah talked. Ma always says he wears his heart on his sleeve for Sarah. His sleeves look like regular sleeves to me. Once I asked what it meant. "It means he dotes on her, Rebecca," Pa explained, but I still looked puzzled.

"Sarah is eighteen and Lucas is thirty-four," Ma added. "He has already made his mark in business and he can afford to spoil her, so he does."

She gave a little sigh of happiness and smiled at Pa. He winked back. They have been married a lot longer than my aunt and uncle and they have had me for eight years. I don't think they dote on each other, but anyone with eyes can see they love each other. They love my aunt and uncle, too, just as I do. Aunt Sarah is pretty and kind, and Uncle Lucas is nice and generous.

He built a home for us right across the road from his big brick house,

3

so we can keep Aunt Sarah company when he goes traveling on business. He said Franklinton needs a good lawyer like Pa and he has helped him get started in this brand new town. Pa says Uncle Lucas . . . I felt my head bob forward. It was past my bedtime and I was nodding off to sleep.

"I win!" shouted Aunt Sarah and I jerked awake.

Pa picked me up and carried me across the dirt road. Ma held his arm and stepped carefully, holding the lantern. It was dark and sometimes when we walked home we heard wildcats screech. Once a wolf ran across the road in front of us. Ma said when Aunt Sarah came here as a new bride she was scared to go outside by herself. She had brought two slaves with her from her family's home in Kentucky. Until we arrived, she never went outside without one of them by her side. Did I mention there were a lot of snakes?

Aunt Sarah said she was lonesome and scared until we moved here two years after she did. That's when she learned to shoot a rifle. She became nearly as good a shot as Ma and stopped being such a scaredy cat. Ma said having a young 'un would make Sarah even more brave. She said even a timid mother will do most anything to protect her baby.

As things turned out, Aunt Sarah soon had two babies to protect and care for. No, they were not twins. How she got the second one is a strange and amazing tale, which I will get to in a minute. (Pa says I can tell a good tale but I take too long to get to the point. Ma says it's all the little details that make my stories lively.)

All I can say is, you would not expect what happened to come to pass

4

here in the Ohio wilderness. But wait! I must first tell what Uncle Lucas did before his son William Starling Sullivant was born.

There were no doctors in Franklinton, so he fetched one all the way from Chillicothe! Uncle Lucas was not exactly sure when the baby would come, so he brought the doctor three weeks ahead of time. Ma tried to tell him it wasn't time yet. Aunt Sarah's belly was still sticking out straight in front of her and had not yet dropped down low. But Uncle Lucas said he did not want to take any chances with his Sarah.

The doctor saw right away that Sarah was a few weeks away from birthing. He tried not to act irritated, but everyone could tell he was. Finally, though, he fell to playing whist with them in the evenings and reading his medical books in the daytime. Time must have crept by like a mouse, but I suspect Uncle Lucas was paying him more than he ever got for delivering an ordinary Chillicothe baby.

Finally, on January 15, 1803—after a good bit of screaming from Aunt Sarah—William Starling Sullivant was born. They would not let me in her house while she was birthing but I heard her from our house across the road.

I bet you are wondering about that second baby I mentioned. Well, he arrived at Aunt Sarah's house a few days after William was born. A man named Arthur Boke brought him. Mr. Boke was a traveling surveyor who sometimes worked for Uncle Lucas. He helped him measure out different plots of land for where buildings and such would go in Franklinton.

The baby was squalling real loud—and no wonder! Even I could tell he was hungry. He kept thrashing his little head around. He was wrapped

in an old rag. See, his mother did not want him or could not keep him. Some people said Aunt Sarah's woman slave was his mother. That could be. She ran off a little while before Arthur Boke brought the baby to my uncle. No one ever sat me down and told me the facts. I just hung around and kept quiet, hoping to hear the details. (I truly believe it's the details that make any tale a good one.) Whenever they noticed me listening, Ma and Aunt Sarah hushed up about the one baby—Arthur—and talked about William instead. Still, I managed to hear more than they wanted me to.

As near as I could piece together, Arthur Boke was the baby's father. Because he traveled all over doing surveying work, he could not keep the baby. He did not know what to do with it, so he brought it to Uncle Lucas.

Uncle Lucas didn't know what to do, either. But Aunt Sarah did. "That baby is hungry," she said. "Give him to me."

She shooed the men outside and sat down with him in the rocking chair beside William's cradle. Her mother's milk had come in a couple of days before. "Right on schedule," Ma had told her cheerfully.

Aunt Sarah put the motherless baby to her breast and nursed him with her own milk. Later, she told Ma that he quieted down and snuggled into her arms like he felt right at home. And that is just where he was, for Aunt Sarah and Uncle Lucas took him in and raised him. They named him Arthur Boke, Jr. and, as near as I could tell, they treated him just as fine as they treated everybody else in the Sullivant family.

Oh, some folks gossiped about a white woman raising a Negro child.

6

But Aunt Sarah paid them no mind. Uncle Lucas was a rich man and the founder of Franklinton. Most people in town owed him in one way or another. Nobody was foolish enough to say anything directly to my aunt or uncle.

So that is how my Aunt Sarah and Uncle Lucas came to raise the first Negro child born in Franklinton. Aunt Sarah birthed two more sons and a daughter. She died in 1814 of typhus, a terrible disease she got when she took care of some sick soldiers stationed at an army camp in Franklinton.

We all cried our eyes out over the loss of our dear Sarah. No one wept harder than Arthur, the son who had come in through her front door and moved into her heart.

Arthur Boke, Jr. lived with the Sullivants until his death in 1841 and was buried in the Sullivant family plot in Franklinton Cemetery. The inscription on his tombstone, written by the Sullivant family, reads in part:
"He was Nursed, Nourished By Sarah Sullivant With Her Children Among Whom He Lived Respected Till the End of His Life. He Died August 10, 1841."

Sarah Sullivant was only 33 years old when she died. Arthur Boke, Jr. was 38. Today, we would consider both these people to be "too young to die."

In the 1800s, early death happened all too often. Many women developed infections after childbirth. They died soon after their babies were born. Like Sarah, many men and women died of typhus, smallpox and other contagious diseases. No one knew what germs were until 1861. That's when Louis Pasteur published his work on germ theory. In 1878, Robert Koch figured out that germs caused wounds to become infected.

Those lucky enough to live a long life usually did so without help from doctors. Home remedies were popular. Here are two. They don't sound very appealing, do they?

Cough Syrup: Chop up a large onion into very small pieces. Cover it with sugar and let the sugar soak in overnight. Add a tablespoon of water. Let it soak. Then throw out the onion and drink the water.

Stomach Ache: Heat bear fat until it turns into warm grease. Rub it on the stomach. Wrap a warm flannel cloth around yourself. Then lie down and try to rest.

A Gift From the Wyandot

"Jane, I need you to rake the coals from the oven," Aunt Mary called. "It's hot enough to put in the cornbread, and I want to get it baked before we work in the garden."

I put little Keziah Hamlin in her cradle. Then I scampered out to the yard. Aunt Mary stood beside the brick oven Uncle Nathaniel had built. "Take care not to scrape the coals near your clothes," she warned.

I poked carefully with a long stick, knocking the coals away from my feet. Meanwhile, Aunt Mary spread the cornbread batter on a thin board. Just as she shoved it into the oven, we heard a wail from inside.

"Time to nurse the baby," she said. "Keep an eye on the oven for me."

"I'll keep an eye out for the Indians, too," I said. "I know how they love to take your cornbread."

"Shush, Jane!" she scolded, as she went into the cabin to feed Keziah. "The Wyandot don't look at it that way. They believe it is a trade, and leave a piece of venison in return."

It was peaceful in the yard. I was glad to be outside and free of chores for a few minutes. I loved my Aunt Mary and Uncle Nathaniel, but life in Ohio was not as pleasant as it was in New Jersey.

There, I lived with my family in a small settlement. I had big brothers, little sisters, and an eight-year-old neighbor girl to play with. Here, there are no neighbors—unless you count the Indian village near the Scioto River. I get lonely sometimes, but my aunt and uncle act like living here is a grand adventure.

Uncle Nathaniel loves to boast that their cabin is the first of many.

11

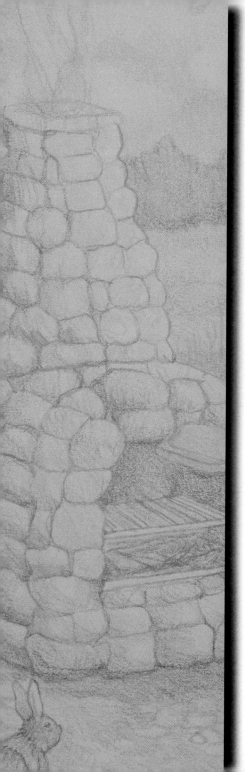

"I expect that a big town will grow up on the banks of the Scioto, Jane. Mark my words," he often says, "it will become quite a busy place. You may decide to stay on, marry, and raise your own family here."

I did not think so, but I smiled politely. My mother had sent me to stay for six months to help Aunt Mary with her baby. Tending Keziah has been the best part of my visit. She is beautiful! She has bright blue eyes and blonde hair the color of corn silk. She is healthy, too, and sweet-tempered. She smiles at everyone who picks her up.

I hear a rustling in the woods. Indians! It's a warm day, but the hair on my arms stands up. I run toward the cabin just as a deer walks into the clearing. Whew! A deer doesn't scare me. If Uncle Nathaniel were here, that deer would become our supper. He is fishing at the river.

Enough daydreaming. Inside, Aunt Mary is singing to Keziah. Out here, the cornbread smells crispy. It's time to pull it out of the oven.

Last week I set the cornbread on a stump to cool before going inside to tend Keziah. The squirrels and other critters ate it before you could say "Jack Robinson." Uncle Nathaniel and Aunt Mary had a good laugh. But we all love cornbread and they would not find it funny the second time.

"Thank you, Jane," Aunt Mary calls as I pull the cornbread from the oven. "Slide it onto this plate and carry it inside."

"The critters will hate to see it go," I joked. "No supper for them tonight."

I set the plate on the table and glanced out the open window. Keziah is lying on a quilt under a shade tree. Aunt Mary is holding two hoes and one of them is for me. Goody!

Next to tending Keziah, I enjoy gardening best. I like the smell of the dirt and the feel of the sun warming my clothes. In a few weeks, the vegetables we are planting today will appear like magic.

Of course, I know there is no magic to it—just a lot of hard work. Uncle Nathaniel says settlers here have learned a lot from the Indians. He says if you haven't learned to trap and skin your own food or grow it in the ground, you will go hungry.

Aunt Mary and I work in the garden, planting potatoes, beans and tomatoes. Every once in a while, we stop to drink a dipperful of cold water.

"Keziah looks ready for another nap," I say.

Aunt Mary nods. "Will you take her inside and put her in her cradle, Jane? She'll sleep better in there."

I pick Keziah up and kiss her neck. "I had better change her diaper first," I say, "even her booties are wet."

Inside, I pin a clean diaper on Keziah and take off her booties. Sometimes she likes to be rocked, but I will not need to do that today. Her eyes are falling shut as I tuck her into the cradle.

The smell of the cornbread makes my mouth water. I would love to cut a piece for myself, but mama told me to use my company manners while I am here. I pinch a little bite off the edge where it won't be noticed and go back outside to hoe some more.

Aunt Mary is young and she can be a lot of fun. As we work, we sing silly songs as loud as we can. Every once in a while, Aunt Mary puts her finger to her lips and we cock our ears toward the cabin.

"Not a peep from Keziah," I say, a couple of hours later. "She has taken another long nap. I hope she will sleep tonight."

"So do I," agrees Aunt Mary. "We are about finished out here. Let me knock the dirt from our hoes while you get her up from her nap. Then I'll nurse her before I start supper."

I trot toward the cabin, thinking I will take another little pinch off the edge of the cornbread. I might even cut myself a piece.

The plate is still setting on the table, but the cornbread is gone. My heart beats so fast that I can feel it in my throat. I stand as still as a rock. My eyes search the small cabin. "Who's here?" I whisper. Then I say louder, "Is somebody here?"

Then it hits me. Keziah! I rush to her cradle and find it empty. "Aunt Mary!" I scream. "Aunt Mary! Keziah is gone! So is the cornbread."

Aunt Mary is beside me in a second. Her eyes dart around the room. She puts her hand into the cradle. "It's cold," she says.

I fall to the floor with a sob. "There's not time to cry, Jane," Aunt Mary says, wiping own her eyes. "The Indians took Keziah a while ago. Otherwise, her bed would still be warm from the heat of her body."

Aunt Mary puts on her bonnet and hands mine to me. "We must find Nathaniel. Then we will all go to the Wyandot village and ask them to give Keziah back."

I feel scared. What if the Indians capture us, too?

We hold hands and try to peer through the trees. Maybe Keziah is nearby.

Tears run down my face, but Aunt Mary looks brave and determined.

14

"Nathaniel says the Indians here are not unfriendly," she says. "He says they are just curious. We may be the first white people they have ever seen."

I sniff and brush away my tears. "They have probably never seen a yellow-haired baby before," I add. "Maybe they . . ."

Suddenly, two Indians appear from the woods and walk softly toward us. One carries a piece of venison. The other carries Keziah. Aunt Mary grips my hand in warning. She does not need to warn me. I am too scared to talk.

I watch as the taller Indian lays a piece of venison on the

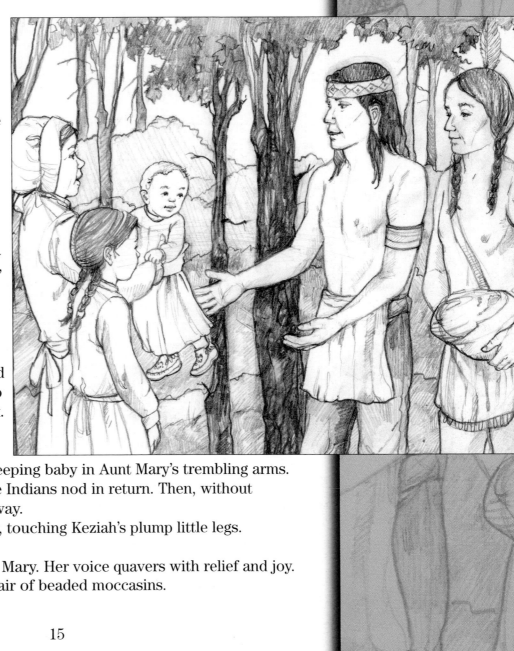

ground. The other places the sleeping baby in Aunt Mary's trembling arms. She nods and tries to smile. The Indians nod in return. Then, without speaking, they turn and walk away.

"Look, Aunt Mary," I whisper, touching Keziah's plump little legs. "The Indians gave her a gift."

"So they did!" exclaims Aunt Mary. Her voice quavers with relief and joy.

On Keziah's tiny feet are a pair of beaded moccasins.

15

That is how the first white baby born east of the Scioto River came to own a beautiful pair of moccasins. Of course, Keziah outgrew them before I returned to New Jersey. Secretly, I hoped Aunt Mary would give them to me to help me remember the scariest thing that happened during my visit.

I think she might have, too, if it hadn't been for Uncle Nathaniel and his grand ideas. He wrapped up those moccasins and put them away in a dresser drawer. He was sure a big town would spring up near the Scioto River. Someday, he said, folks would want to see Keziah's little moccasins and hear the tale of how she got them.

Mary and Nathaniel Hamlin came to Ohio from New Jersey in 1800. Theirs was one of the few cabins in the area that is now Columbus. Keziah Hamlin was born in 1804, one year after Ohio became a state.

Life was hard. There were no neighbors nearby and Mary was probably lonely. She would not have had much time for visitors, though. Like other pioneer women, she was busy from sunrise until sunset. Besides cooking, cleaning, and taking care of her child, she also:
• planted and tended a vegetable garden,
• raised chickens and milked the cow,·
• churned butter,
• made candles and soap,
• wove cloth and sewed the family's clothes,
• "doctored" the family with teas made from roots and herbs she gathered,
• helped her husband with his chores.

16

My Family Hides Runaway Slaves

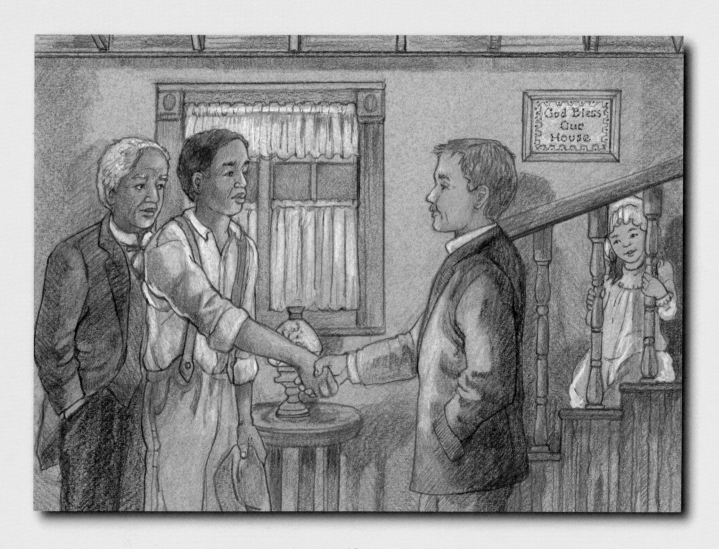

I used to think grownups were a puzzle—especially my father, Jason Bull. He is the preacher at the Methodist Chapel in Clintonville. Father says because he is a preacher his daughters must live up to a higher standard. He says we must be always be truthful.

Then I noticed something. Where slavery is concerned, Father himself does not tell the truth—at least, not the whole truth. Oh, he tells it from the pulpit. He says it goes against our beliefs to hold Negroes in bondage because we are all equal.

A few folks frown when he says this, but most of them nod and agree. The Methodists are mainly abolitionists. They think slavery is wrong and want to give Negroes the same freedom as whites. This sounds fair to me. My goodness! It is 1851 and by now we should know better than to treat Negroes like slaves. All people have the right to be free and treated equally with kindness and respect.

When I told Father my thoughts, I could tell he was proud of me. "That is a good way to think about it, Elizabeth. Slavery is a blot on our nation's character. We must hope that white people are moved to release all Negroes from bondage."

My father does more than talk about slavery. I have heard men come to our house late at night when my sisters and I are upstairs in bed. Mother slips them in through the back door and they go into Father's study.

I used to creep out of bed and look. The late-night visitors are Negroes. I heard Mother call them by name. One is Mr. Lewis Washington, who delivers wood to burn in the furnace of our church. He wears work clothes

and is very tall and strong. Another one is Mr. Poindexter who preaches at the Second Baptist Church. Another Negro man named John Ward sometimes visits, too. They don't stay long and they talk to Father in low voices.

When I asked Mother about these visits, she grabbed my shoulders and stared deep into my eyes. "I cannot tell you anything, Elizabeth. Do not ask your father, either," she said. "And for heaven's sake, do not tell anyone you have seen these men in our house."

"Why not?" I asked.

"Telling others could put our family in danger," she said. "Your father and I are doing good work. That's all you need to know."

A thrill of pride ran through my body. I knew from what Mother didn't say that our house was a stop on the Underground Railroad. I promised her I would stop snooping and that I wouldn't tell anyone anything. I kept the second part of the promise. I didn't keep the first part.

I had never seen or heard a runaway slave at our house. It is not very big and there really is no place to hide. We have no basement and no attic. My sisters share a bedroom with me. My parents sleep in the other bedroom.

One evening, I figured it out. I had said my prayers and was looking out the window before crawling into bed. My little sisters were already asleep. I saw Mr. Washington's wagon pull up behind the church, which is right next to our house. The wagon was piled high with wood. There was already plenty of wood behind the church. Why did we need more?

20

Mr. Washington got out and looked around. Then he began unloading the wood and stacking it around the basement door. He was as slow as molasses. Why was it taking him so long? Then, the moon slid behind a cloud and I saw two people crawl from the heap of wood in his wagon. Like dark shadows, they slipped through an opening in the church woodpile. I blinked and they were gone.

Soon, I heard Mother go downstairs. I wondered if she was fixing something for the runaways to eat. I fell asleep before I found out.

I had never seen a runaway slave. The two I saw cast small shadows. Were they children? It was all so exciting! But I knew better than to go poking around. I did not want to lead anyone to the hiding spot. I vowed to keep my eyes open and my mouth shut.

I hoped that my parents would be able to help the slaves get to their promised land—Canada—where they would be free. Folks caught helping slaves escape were sent to prison. If my parents were caught, what would happen to my sisters and me? I soon had reason to worry.

The next morning, slave hunters burst into the church. Father was in his office there, writing a sermon. Mother and I were in our home next door, sewing bonnets. My sisters were napping upstairs.

"Federal marshals!" we heard them shout through our open window. "We have a warrant to search your church and your home for runaway slaves!"

Mother's eyes darted back and forth. I could almost see her mind working out a plan. She handed the bonnets to me.

"Slip out the back door with these, Elizabeth. Take them to the woodpile

behind the church," she said. "Stick your hand through the hole in the woodpile and rap three times on the window."

I nodded and showed no surprise. She realized then that I knew the runaways were hiding in the church basement.

"Put the bonnets on their heads," she added, "and bring the girls around to the back door."

"But what—" I began.

"No questions, Elizabeth! Go now!" she said sharply.

I took the bonnets and slipped out. I could hear Father talking, trying to stall the men as they searched the choir loft. I figured he had taken them as far away from the runaways as he could.

Meantime, I tapped on the basement window. Two scared, dark faces appeared. I motioned for the girls to push the window up and crawl out through the woodpile. Before they could scramble to their feet, I put a bonnet on each and tied the strings under their chins. The wide brims hid their faces. I grabbed their hands and together we scurried 50 feet to our back door. Mother was standing inside with long white nightgowns that she buttoned on over their ragged clothes.

Then she knelt before them and held their hands. "Elizabeth is going to take you upstairs and tuck you both into my big bed," she explained. "She is going to cover you with blankets. Leave your bonnets on, pull the blankets up, and keep your faces turned toward the wall. Do not make a sound and do not move until Elizabeth comes to get you. Do you understand?"

22

"Yes, M'am," the girls replied, their eyes wide with fear.

"The Lord is watching over you," Mother assured them. "Do not be afraid. You will soon be on your way to the next safe house, where your mother is waiting."

The girls and I crept upstairs. After they crawled into my parents' bed, I pulled off their shoes and stuck them under the pillows. I covered them with the thick bedspread and tucked it up around their ears. It was not safe to talk— I did not want to wake my sisters—but I squeezed their hands before I left.

I had scarcely gotten back downstairs when Father and the slave hunters walked into the front door. They looked irritated. I thought they must be disappointed not to have found anyone but Father in the church.

"These gentlemen need to search our home, Mary," Father said to Mother.

He spoke politely, as though they were curious houseguests. The men looked ill at ease. They seemed ashamed to search a minister's home.

Mother was as gracious as Father. "Look all you want, gentlemen," she said. "But I must warn you that I have four children upstairs with chickenpox. The two little ones in the back bedroom are doing better. The girls in the front bedroom are still contagious."

The men looked alarmed. "Chicken pox is a miserable disease for children," Mother added, "but it can be deadly for adults. I hope you have both already had it."

The taller man nervously scratched his hand. "I can't recall whether I have or not," he said.

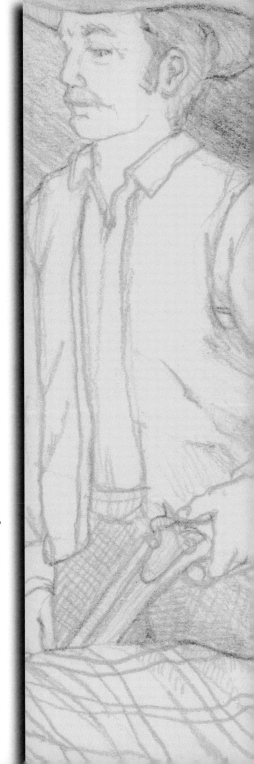

"Neither can I," said the other man, pulling his partner's arm. "Come on. We'll check downstairs first and then make a quick look through the bedrooms."

"If you could do it quietly, gentlemen, I would appreciate it," Mother said. "The children are worn out. They're napping."

It took them only a few minutes to look through our small kitchen, dining room, and sitting room. They opened cupboards. They thumped walls for hollow hiding places. They felt along the floor for trap doors.

Mother, Father, and I sat and watched politely. When they found nothing, Mother said, "Elizabeth, would you please lead the gentlemen upstairs?

24

I don't want the girls to be frightened if they wake up and see strangers in their rooms."

Suddenly, I got a flash of inspiration. I took off my shoes. Mother covered her mouth to hide her smile. Father's eyes crinkled. The men followed my example. They took off their heavy boots and we all tiptoed upstairs.

Then, barely breathing, they looked under the beds and inside the closets. They did not knock on the walls or feel along the floor. They were so scared of chicken pox germs that they hardly glanced at the girls in the beds. My little sisters did not wake up and the runaways, heaped with blankets, did not move.

When we came back downstairs, I handed the slave hunters their boots. Father shook their hands. Mother gave them a sack filled with cold chicken and biscuits. They were grateful for the food and very glad to leave.

My little sisters still do not know about the many runaways who find food and shelter in our church basement as they travel north to Canada. They do not know that James Preston Poindexter directs the actions of Negro members of the Underground Railroad, or that Father supervises the whole operation. They have no idea that Lewis Washington delivers anything but wood in his wagon, or that John Ward leads runaways out of Columbus to the next stop on their journey. Someday, when all the slaves are free, I will tell them.

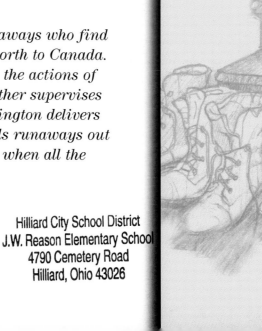

25

Ohio was the first step to freedom for many slaves. Thousands passed through on their way to Canada. The state was strongly against slavery. There were 229 antislavery groups operating in Ohio before the Civil War. Most were connected in some way with the Underground Railroad.

The Underground Railroad did not operate under the ground, and it wasn't a real railroad. It was a huge network of paths and trails that led runaway slaves to "safe" houses like Reverend Bull's home in Clintonville.

Because so many people helped the slaves travel north to Canada, Congress passed a law in 1850 to help their owners get them back. Slaves were considered "property." They could be bought, sold, and traded like horses. The Fugitive Slave Act permitted federal marshals to find slaves and return them to their owners. The Act also said those who helped slaves escape could be fined and put into prison.

James Preston Poindexter, John Ward, and Lewis Washington and other free Negroes risked their lives helping slaves escape. Jason Bull and his family risked their own freedom. It was not unusual for ministers who were caught to be put in jail to "set an example" to the members of their churches.

Columbus has a long history of racial cooperation. We should be proud of the part our city played in helping runaway slaves.

Our Journey From Germany

Mutti says we will get our land legs back when we reach Columbus. We have had mostly sea legs since we left Germany, many weeks ago. I learned to walk on the sailing ship, but *Mutti* did not. She stumbled and swayed. She grabbed onto things to keep her balance. She sipped tea all day to settle her stomach and hoped the time would pass quickly.

Poor *Mutti!* She says she is grateful that her children did not feel seasick. She is even more grateful to be gliding slowly in a small boat on the Ohio and Erie Canal instead of being tossed about on a ship in the Atlantic Ocean.

My sister Louise is glad, too. She likes the canal boat but can hardly wait until we arrive. "How much longer, Carl?" she asks me. "When will we see *Vater?*"

She asks me the same question ten times a day. I try to be kind. *Vater* is already living in Columbus. I am nine years old but must act as the man in the family. *Mutti* always seems to be sick and I must look after Louise. It is difficult! When she is not asking when we will arrive, Louise is begging me to tell her the story of our journey. She is only six and wants to hear it the same way each time.

"When we see *Vater*, we will have traveled on this many kinds of ships," I say, holding up four fingers. "After we left our home in Germany we took a steam ship down the Rhine River. Then we got on a sailing ship called the British Queen . . ."

"That took many weeks!" Louise interrupted. "*Mutti* was sick and I wasn't and you weren't, either. But it sometimes smelled bad."

"That's right," I replied. "We were six long weeks cooped up on the sailing ship. Then we finally docked into New York's harbor and went to Ellis Island. That's where . . . "

"It was loud and noisy!" Louise exclaimed. "The lines of people were so long! All the screaming babies! And the grumbling grownups! And I hated it when the government people poked in our hair to see if we had lice. Ach! Finally, they told us we could stay in America. I was glad when we got onto that other boat."

"So was I," I said, giving her shoulder a little pat.

"And then we got on this canal boat and here we are!" exclaimed Louise. "Carl, when will we see *Vater?*"

"Low bridge—everybody down!" shouted the helmsman.

Louise and I, along with a dozen other people, flattened ourselves on the roof of the canal boat. If we hadn't we would have been knocked off—or at least knocked senseless. *Mutti* made us promise to listen to the helmsman—the man at the front of the boat—and lie down when we were told to.

It was scary the first time. Now we are used to it. It is grand to be outside. The little towns and farms along the canal remind me of Germany.

I am glad *Vater* settled in Ohio instead of in New York City.

He wrote to tell us New York was not clean and pretty like our town in Germany. Instead, it was crowded and dirty. He wrote that there were too many grocery stores in New York. In Columbus, he had heard there were not so many, so that's where he went. He says it was a good choice. There are many Germans in Columbus and most of them live near one another. *Vater*

30

opened a store in the German area. He wrote that we will soon feel right at home in our rooms over the store.

My thoughts and my eyes have wandered from Louise. She has not asked me when we will see *Vater*. She has sneaked away while I was daydreaming. "Louise!" I call. "Louise!"

I scramble to my knees and look for her. She is not on the roof. I do not see her on the deck below. *Gutt* grief! Where is my little sister? She is a headstrong child. Where has she gone?

The boat has stopped moving. It stops at the towns along the canals to trade off the tired mule pulling the boat for one that is rested. This gives people a chance to leave the boat and stretch their legs. I hope Louise did not get off alone. She was napping the last time we swapped mules. She was mad that she had not seen the swap. My eyes scan the backs of the crowd. I see Louise with *Mutti*. They are looking at the roof. Searching for me, most likely. Thank goodness she is safe!

They wait for me to join them on dry land. Before I can scold Louise, she grabs my hand. "Carl, look! Let us go and see the mule. *Mutti* says I can go if you come, too."

"Forgive me, *Mutti*," I say. "I do not know how Louise got away from me."

"It is all right, Carl," she replied with a tired smile. "Louise needed to use the toilet and she also needed to see her *mutti*.

"Now, she needs to see the mule," *Mutti* added. "Louise is a girl with many needs. Perhaps you will help her with this need while I look in the shops during our brief stop."

31

"Of course," I reply, taking Louise's hand. "We will go and ask the hoggee."
"Not hoggee!" Louise said, stamping her foot. "I want to see the mule."
"Do you see the boy there with the mule?" I asked. "He is called the hoggee and he is the boss of the mule."

Louise looked impressed. *Mutti* smiled and waved us off. She walked slowly. Her legs were still wobbly from the sailing ship. Louise and I ran to the path where the hoggee stood harnessing the fresh mule. He could not speak German and we did not speak English. But I used my hands to show that Louise wanted to pet the mule.

He scratched his nose and motioned Louise to the front of the mule. Then he gave her an apple to feed it. The mule nipped it from her hand, its lips barely brushing her palm.

Louise was delighted. *"Gutt! Gutt!"* she shouted. The hoggee grinned, showing some missing baby teeth. "He is not much older than I am," I thought. "He has a big job for a young boy."

Mutti called to us that it was time to board the boat. *"Danke!"* I said, giving a slight bow to the hoggee.

"I don't want to go!" Louise exclaimed. "I want to stay with the mule and his boss."

The hoggee did not have to understand German to know that Louise did not want to get on the boat. He pointed to us both, then to himself, and then moved his feet. It was leafy and green on the towpath. The air smelled good. The boy and the mule seemed friendly. I would ask *Mutti.*

She looked uncertain. Then I ticked off on my fingers the reasons for saying "yes." One, we were in no danger. Two, she could see us from the boat. Three, we would be walking only four miles an hour.

Mutti nodded as she listened. Then she smiled. Her eyes danced with mischief. "You have convinced me, Carl. You may do it," she said. "And I can give you one more reason. Our next—and last—stop is Columbus."

Louise jumped up and down. "Won't *Vater* be surprised to see us walking in?" she asked.

It was fun to walk beside the hoggee and his mule. Their names, he told us, were "John" and "Harriet." We took off our shoes and dug our toes into the towpath's soft, cool dirt. The hoggee and I whistled. Louise sang to Harriet. Harriet snorted softly as she pulled the boat along the canal. *Mutti* waved from the boat.

It was a wonderful way to end our journey.

This story is loosely based on the journey of Mrs. Charlotte Lindenberg and her children. In 1850, they left their small town near Berlin, Germany to join her husband, Theodore, in Columbus.

It took the Lindenbergs six weeks on a sailing ship to travel from Germany to New York. Soon after they arrived, steam ships began making the trip in only two weeks. This led more and more Germans to settle in America. Between 1820 and 1920, nearly five and a half million Germans settled in the U.S. Now, 58 million people in America have relatives who came here from Germany.

Germans have had a big influence our American way of life. Here are a few of the many things they brought us or taught us:

• Santa Claus—the Germans called him "Kris Kringle."
• Christmas trees—early ones were decorated with candles.
• Frankfurters—we call them "hot dogs."
• Hamburgers—they came from the German city of Hamburg.
• Blue jeans—the first pair was sewn in the 19th century by German immigrant Levi Strauss.
• Fairy tales—Snow White, Sleeping Beauty, and other tales were written by two German brothers whose last name was "Grimm."
• Classical music and folk music—Germans founded many of our country's symphony orchestras.

When Mr. Lincoln Came to Town

"Listen!" I shouted. "I can hear Mr. Lincoln's train."

"Pick up your feet and hurry along, Nathaniel," Pa urged me. "It's nearly 2 o'clock. Half the folks in Columbus are on their way to the depot and the other half are already there."

He grabbed my hand and we set off at a dead run. The train whistle blew again and everybody else took off running, too. I am glad my pa is young and strong and long-legged. I had to take three steps for each one of his. I was proud that I kept up with him.

I wanted to tell him this. I couldn't talk, though. I was panting like an old hound dog. My breath puffed before my face like steam from a steam engine. My nose felt as cold as the steel on the train tracks and my heart pounded like Pa's big hammer.

I could hardly wait to see the new President up close and hear what he had to say. Pa had shown me a likeness of Mr. Lincoln in the newspaper. I knew he was a big tall man and my ma said he had a way with words.

"That man could coax a song out of a hen," Ma had said that morning as she rocked my baby sister. "Maybe he can keep the South from leaving the union."

Ma was real sad not to be with us but Mandy is too new to go out into crowds. She is no bigger than a jackrabbit, but she makes a whole lot more noise. She . . .

Suddenly Pa stopped running and yanked me over his head and up onto his shoulders. Everyone began to clap, even my Pa, and I thought I would fall. Thousands of people jostled one another and pushed to see the President.

On my perch, I was taller than anyone. I am sure I got the first look when Mr. Lincoln came out and stood on the platform at the end of the train.

The other men with him had on tall hats but Mr. Lincoln's head was bare. Even so, he stood taller than their hats. He looked like a giant to me—a kind giant with deep, dark eyes and thick black hair and big long ears. His face seemed calm and tired.

Pa had told me Mr. Lincoln's train had left his home in Springfield, Illinois two days before. He had already stopped in Indianapolis and Cincinnati. He was most likely sick of trains—and people, too—but he did not act like it. He waved and seemed glad to see us all.

Mr. Lincoln did not say anything, but one of the tall-hatted men did. "Governor Dennison will receive the President-elect at the Executive rooms," he said, puffing out his skinny chest. "Then Lieutenant Governor Kirk will present him to the general assembly."

I leaned over and whispered to Pa: "What is that scrawny little man saying? When will we get to meet Mr. Lincoln?"

Pa slumped his shoulders. I could not see his face but I felt sure he was disappointed, too. He had read in the paper that the President would meet up with regular folks in Columbus.

The little man kept talking about executive this and assembly that. Finally he said something that made Pa straighten up. "Then the President-elect will proceed to the rotunda of the Capitol, where he will receive the citizens until 5 o'clock P.M."

Pa set me down and commenced to pulling me through the crowd.

"Maybe we can beat this mob back to the State House and do more than look," Pa said. "'Receive the citizens' means he will shake hands with regular folks."

Pa and I pushed through the mob on High Street and then Pa pulled me off through some alleys. I was glad because I could see daylight in front of me instead of men's trousers.

We found us a good spot and waited. It was too cold to sit on the ground. We leaned against a post beside the State House steps. Pa pulled a dishrag from his coat pocket and opened it.

"Biscuits!" I shouted and took two.

"Your ma said she did not want her boys to go hungry," Pa said with a smile. "We don't want our guts rumbling when we meet Mr. Lincoln."

We waited and we waited and we waited some more. Pa said Mr. Lincoln was talking to the big-wigs. Finally, a man opened the doors to the State House and Mr. Lincoln came out.

He looked even more tired than before. The big-wigs must have plumb wore him out. People commenced to cheering and stomping and whistling. Mr. Lincoln smiled and nodded. Then he held up the palms of his hands, like he was giving us all a blessing.

"Ladies and Gentlemen," Mr. Lincoln said. "I thank you for this very kind reception. I do not find strength to repeat my speech to you. I am thankful that you have appeared here to give me this greeting. It is not much to me, for I shall very soon pass away from you. But we have a large country and a large future before us. The manifestations of good will towards the government and affection for the union . . . are of immense value to you . . . I thank you most heartily."

With that, Mr. Lincoln waved again and went inside. The little scrawny man jumped out and said, "Mr. Lincoln will now shake hands in the rotunda with all who desire to meet him."

People poured into the building like water from a jug. "Keep tight hold of my hand, Nathaniel," Pa yelled. "Your ma would not forgive me if I lost you in this mob."

I reckon Pa was afraid I would get knocked from his shoulders. Or else he did not have time to pick me up before the mob took over. I could not see much except men's trousers and ladies' skirts.

I yanked on Pa's hand. "Tell me what you see!" I demanded.

Pa grinned. "I see a bunch of people acting the fool," he replied. "A man is treating Mr. Lincoln's arm like an axe. He keeps swinging it up and down. The scrawny man is trying to pull him off the President."

"What else?" I begged.

"A woman over there just swooned over. It looks like she is about to faint from excitement," Pa said. "Her daughter is fanning her with her hand, trying to help her catch her breath."

"I want to see that, Pa! I want to tell Ma what a swoon looks like."

A space opened up in front of me. I shook loose from Pa's hand and darted through. In a minute, I would see the swooning woman up close.

But I could not see anything. The crowd surged around me and when I turned back, Pa was not there. "Pa! Pa!" I yelled.

Everybody was packed tight together and I could not lean my head back to look for Pa's face. I looked down instead to catch sight of his

40

shoes and britches. The crowd pushed forward and I thought I had found Pa. I grabbed onto a man's leg, but it was not Pa's. He shook me loose without a word and I fell down.

I feared I would be trampled and Ma would be mad. Before I could scramble to my feet, I felt someone lift me by my arms.

"Pa!" I said, before I looked up.

Mr. Lincoln smiled. "I have a son named Willie who is about your size," he said. "What is your name, young man?"

He gripped me close to his side with one hand and continued shaking folks' hands with the other.

"I am Nathaniel Johnson, sir, and I am real glad to meet you," I said. I did not feel one bit scared of the President.

Lincoln laughed. It was a true laugh that made his face crinkle. "I am real glad to meet you, too," he said. "Let me shake your hand."

He leaned down to take hold of my hand. It was a far piece, for Mr. Lincoln was even taller than my Pa. As he pumped my arm, the crowd moved toward the President like dogs after a rabbit and nearly knocked us to the floor.

Mr. Lincoln looked alarmed. "I have had enough of this, Nathaniel!" he exclaimed. He pulled me up the great staircase behind us and directed the tall-hatted men to block the stairs.

For several minutes, we watched the crowd. I saw Pa just as he realized it was me standing up there with the President. His worried face broke into a grin. He lifted up his arm and waved the dishrag like it was Old Glory.

"I see you have been found," Mr. Lincoln said.

"Yes, sir," I replied. "Would you mind shaking my hand again so my Pa can watch?"

That is how I came to meet Mr. Abraham Lincoln on February 13, 1861 and to shake his hand twice. I never saw him alive again.

He was shot on April 14, 1865 by John Wilkes Booth in Washington, D.C. and died the next morning, just a few days after the end of the Civil War. Pa told me Mr. Lincoln was 56 years old.

Two weeks after he was killed, Ma, Mandy, Pa and I went to a public viewing of Mr. Lincoln's body at the Statehouse. We waited in line with thousands of others to pay our final respects before his funeral train continued on to other cities before making its final stop at a graveyard in Springfield, Illinois.

It was a solemn occasion. Everyone cried—even Pa—for the gentle man who had passed away from us so soon.

Before Mr. Lincoln's body was put on the funeral train, it was displayed at the White House and in the Capitol Rotunda. Thousands of people came to pay their respects. Among them were many freed slaves. Historians say Mr. Lincoln's final journey was grandest funeral in the history of the world.

We Arrived

on the Orphan Train

Hazel grips my hand so hard my knuckles hurt. I know she's scared because she will not look at me or at anybody else.

Hazel is only six. When she is scared she stares at her feet. Right now, she is fixing to stare holes in her new shoes.

"Do you see how our shoes look just the same, Hazel?" I ask in a fake cheerful voice. "They match, don't they?"

Hazel nods. Still looking at her feet, she whispers, "Why are we at the train station, Ben? Where are they taking us?"

"We're going on an adventure to find a new home!" I exclaim.

I am not sure this was true. I am repeating what the Children's Aid Society lady said when she took us from the orphanage.

I am the big brother—two years older and six inches taller. I am trying to keep Hazel from crying. If she pitches a fit, one of the Children's Aid ladies might take her from me.

"We have to stay together, and find one home for both of us. Understand?"

Hazel nods again and looks up and down the platform. Every girl wears a blue cotton dress covered by a white pinafore. Every boy wears a white cotton shirt and brown trousers. We all wear brown lace-up shoes. All of us look clean and scared.

About three dozen of us huddle together, waiting to board the last car on the train. It will take us from orphanages in New York City to farm families in the Midwest who will—if we are lucky—take us home with them.

A train clatters into the station and a Children's Aid lady shouts:

45

"Children whose last names begin with A through K, pick up your suitcases and come with me. The rest of you go with Mrs. Reynolds."

"We are named Williams, so we follow her," I say, pointing to Mrs. Reynolds. "Come, Hazel. Pick up your suitcase and remember not to cry."

Mrs. Reynolds helps us stow our suitcases and get settled two across in each seat. She smiles at Hazel and gives each of us a jelly sandwich.

We eat the sandwiches, careful not to drip jelly on our clothes. After the train gets underway, Mrs. Reynolds makes an announcement. "We're bound for Ohio, children, and we'll be on the train for three days," she explains. "Usually we stop at different small towns along the way to introduce you to people looking to adopt. But because we're taking such a small group of children this time, we have advertised only in the Columbus paper. Your new families will come to the courthouse there to see you."

A scrawny red-haired boy calls out, "What happens if we don't get picked?"

"Then you will come back with me again, Oliver, and we'll find you a family on our next trip," Mrs. Reynolds says kindly.

"Do people ever adopt *two* children?" I ask nervously.

"Sometimes they do," she replies. "Each child who's chosen has to agree to go. We'll keep our fingers crossed for you and Hazel."

We are the only brother and sister on the train. Some of the others were separated from their brothers and sisters before they came to the orphanage. Some don't have any family. Some never even knew their parents.

Others, like Hazel and me, were given to the orphanage by their mothers.

46

Our dad ran off right after Hazel was born. Mama had to work all day and there was no one to watch over us. For a while, she visited us every Sunday. Hazel does not remember her at all. I remember that she smelled like soap because she worked at a soap factory.

The clickety-clack of the wheels on the train track makes me sleepy. The wooden seats are hard, so I sit wad up my jacket and sit on it. Then I lean against Hazel. She is my little sleeping pillow.

We pass green fields and trees and a few houses. I wonder what Ohio will look like.

Two days and many jelly sandwiches later, I find out. "We'll soon be in Columbus," Mrs. Reynolds calls. "Time to get ready."

We all wash up and change into fresh clothes. Mrs. Reynolds braids Hazel's hair. Everyone looks excited except Oliver. He looks worried. This is the second time he has ridden the orphan train. I cross my fingers as we get off the train. "Please let us all be picked," I whisper, "and please keep Hazel and me together."

The courthouse is not far from the train station. Our eyes get big as we enter a grand tall building. Silently, we sit at the front of a large room.

"Now, smile and look people in the eye, children, Mrs. Reynolds instructs. "They are choosing you but you must also choose them in return. Don't be too picky, though. It doesn't pay to judge a book by its cover."

I think to myself that is just what they are doing to us—judging us by what we look like. But I know better than to say so. I put on a big smile and grip Hazel's hand so folks know we are together.

"Don't chew on your pigtail, Hazel," I scold, pulling it from her mouth. "You'll get your hair ribbon wet."

A bushy-haired man with a red beard opens the door and pokes his head in. "Can we come in and look them over now?" he asks.

Mrs. Reynolds motions him in and we stare at the people who might decide to take us home. There are tall ones, short ones, fat ones, and thin ones. A few people are dressed up—those must be the ones that live in town. Most of the men are wearing overalls, though, and the women are wearing plain-looking dresses.

The bushy-haired man leads the crowd to where we are sitting. His wife, small and anxious-looking, tugs on his shirt sleeve. "He looks kind of like you, Orville, with his red hair and all," she says.

Oliver pulls his shoulders back and slides to the front of his chair. He looks smack into the man's eyes and shows all his teeth when he smiles.

I close my eyes. When I open them, I see they have taken his hands and are leading him away. Oliver is so happy to have a home that he does not even wave good-bye.

One by one the other children are chosen. Several people comment on how pretty Hazel is and how tall and strong I look. But when they find out we are a pair, nobody wants us.

"No," says Mrs. Reynolds, for the third or fourth time. "Ben and Hazel are brother and sister and they want to stay together. Please think about taking them both."

"I already have a boy," one man says as he moves on.

48

"She's prettier than my own daughter," a woman explains. "It wouldn't do to make my girl jealous."

Finally, every child is gone except for Hazel and me. Mrs. Reynolds struggles to put on a smile.

"Pick up your suitcases, children," she says. "We'll find you a family next time."

I am grateful that Mrs. Reynolds kept her promise and did not separate us. But I am sad that we have to ride the train back to New York.

"Wait! Wait!" demands a woman's voice from the back of the room.

We look up to see a short, plump couple rushing toward us. The woman's face is as plain and round as an oatmeal cookie. The man is clean-shaven and jolly looking.

"We are Mr. and Mrs. Raymond Fellers," he says, shaking Mrs. Reynolds' hand. "We got lost looking for the courthouse."

"We don't have any children," his wife adds.

"When we read about the orphan train, I told Raymond we had to come," she explains, smoothing Hazel's hair.

"Do you like dogs?" Mr. Fellers asks,

"I don't rightly know, sir," I reply. "We don't have pets at the orphanage."

"You'll like Tippy," Mr. Fellers says, taking my hand. "She's a friendly old collie."

Mrs. Reynolds smiles and her eyes fill up with tears.

"It sounds like Mr. and Mrs. Fellers want to take you both," she says. "What do you say, children?"

"Let's go!" Hazel declares. She does not sound a bit shy.

I am too excited to speak. All I can do is nod and smile. This time, my smile is for real.

The orphan trains were the idea of a New Yorker named Charles Loring Brace. Mr. Brace worried about the thousands of homeless children living in the streets. Many stole and others begged to get by.

He was a minister who decided to devote his life to poor children. In 1853, Mr. Brace founded the Children's Aid Society of New York. He sent flyers to cities throughout the Midwest. The flyers announced the day and time an orphan train filled with children available for adoption would arrive.

Some families wanted only another set of hands to work on their farms. Others truly wanted to help a child in need. Others were childless.

There was no charge to take a child. Some children went to wonderful families. Others led miserable lives and left their adoptive families as soon as they were able.

The orphan trains made regular trips from New York to the Midwest between 1854 and 1929. The Children's Aid Society did not keep very good records. However, during the 75 years the trains ran, it's believed that as many as 400,000 orphans found homes.

Mamie's Diary

of the Great Flood

My name is Mamie McCampbell and this is my first diary. I got it for my birthday from my parents, E.F. and Martha McCampbell. I am nine years old and I have two brothers. One is named Thomas and the other is John.

There is a lock on this diary. I hope it will keep them out!

MARCH 23, 1913

Morning Today is Easter Sunday. Mother said it is raining cats and dogs and we will not go out. Usually, she does not let us miss church for anything. Shoot! I wanted to wear my new birthday dress. Thomas and John want me to play cards. Father says, "No cards on Sunday, boys. Read your lessons and then you can play checkers." Mother says I can write in my diary again later. First, I must do my chores. So far, it has been a very dull day.

Afternoon Hello, Diary! We had soup for lunch. John and Thomas would not let me play checkers. I don't care! I would rather write. It is as gray outside as my old wool socks and it is still raining to beat the band.

Our yard is flooded up to the front steps. My father goes out for a walk on Sunday afternoons. He calls his walks "constitutionals." Today he is reading the *Columbus Citizen* newspaper instead. Mother says we all have to stay in the house until the rain stops. I am going to read a book.

Evening Our telephone rang! It hardly ever rings and when it does it is always for Father. We children are not allowed to talk on the telephone and Mother does not like to. Oh my goodness! It is someone from Mount Carmel Hospital. Father looks worried.

When he hangs up, he tells us the water is getting "dangerously" high.

We rush to the window but it is dark and we can't see. My father says he has to get us to safety and then go to the hospital to help. He says high water in the part of Franklinton called the Bottoms makes that neighborhood look like a lake. Sick people there are being taken to the hospital in rowboats. He says one woman had her baby in a boat. Oh my!

I forgot to tell you, Diary—my father is a doctor. Besides caring for sick people, he also works for the governor. He is in charge of the State Board of Health. He says everyone in Columbus is his patient.

He tells us to put on rubber boots and pack warm clothes. He tells my mother to put together a basket of food. He tells my brothers to help him carry our furniture upstairs.

We will go to Avondale School, he says, where we will be safe. Oh my goodness, I am sorry I complained that today was dull. Look what has happened!

MARCH 24, 1913

Morning Dear Diary—a lot can happen in just one day. The water was up past my father's waist last night and the hospital sent a rowboat for us!

Mother, Thomas, John, and I are sleeping on cots at Avondale School with about one hundred other women and children. Mother says we are lucky the furnace is working here. She says to count our blessings, for many people in Columbus are cold and hungry.

Afternoon It is still raining. The provisions boat has come and guess who was on it? Father! He is looking to see if there are extra cots for his patients. The furnace at Mt. Carmel went out. Father says everyone will have to share a cot. That way, there will be twice as many beds—enough for most of the hospital patients. He tells us that most of Ohio and Indiana are flooded. He read us part of a statement from the governor: "The waters have assumed such unknown heights that it will be a miracle if villages and towns are not wiped out of existence in the southern parts of Ohio. My judgment is that there has never been such a tragedy in the history of the republic."

Mother suggests that we hold hands and think about those who are lost. We do. I look out the window. It is still raining.

Evening Some rescue workers come into the school for supper. They are dirty, tired and unhappy. They have gotten news that things are much worse in Dayton and Cincinnati than they are here. "There are dead bodies being washed through the streets of Dayton," one man tells Father. "The Ohio River flooded in Cincinnati and a thousand people are dead."

I am going to lock you up, Diary. I am too sad to write any more.

MARCH 25, 1913

Morning It was hard to sleep last night. The cot is narrow and Mother is large. There is hardly any room for me. I know better than to complain. She

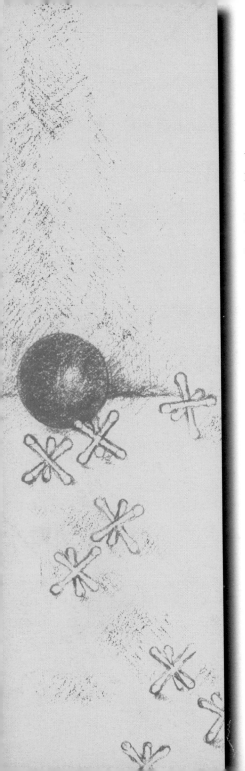

will remind me that Father and many others have had no sleep. She will tell me to count my blessings.

When I woke up a while ago I noticed something wonderful. It has stopped raining! Maybe tonight we will use the tickets Father bought last week for "Little Boy Blue." It is being performed at the Great Southern Hotel and Theater—a grand place. I can wear my birthday dress! Hooray!

Father comes in to wake us up. He has been with patients all night. He says more buildings have been washed away and more people have been hurt or killed. I ask him if the Great Southern is still standing.

He smiles and tells me it is, but that the play will not be performed. "The opera company could not get through the flood waters, " he says. We will celebrate your birthday when they come back, Mamie. I promise."

As we eat, he tells us stories he has heard from the rescue workers. One man clung onto a pole all night until he the rescuers found him. Another family's house fell over and they hung onto the side of the roof until the rescue boats came.

Afternoon Dear Diary—I met a girl named Nellie and we are going to play jacks. I am locking you up for now. John and Thomas are playing cards. They have not tried to read you yet, but I am not taking any chances!

MARCH 26, 1913

Morning Dear Diary—Guess what? Mother has not gotten any smaller and our cot has not gotten any bigger. I want to go home! So does Mother. I can tell her patience is about to wear out. Thomas and John were fighting and she threatened to have Father give them a whipping. I am going to find Nellie and play some more jacks.

There is nothing more to write except for one thing, which I will repeat. I want to go home!

MARCH 27, 1913

Afternoon Dear Diary—Sorry I did not write anything this morning. We were busy packing up. We are going home! Some families are staying here because they have nowhere else to go. Our home is still standing. Hooray! Mother says we must count our blessings.

Everyone is surprised at how fast the water went down. Now the town is covered with mud. Father has issued something called a "sanitation proclamation" to the people of Columbus. He asked Mother to read it to us before it is printed in the newspaper.

It was long and serious. The part I remember is this: "Dead animals should be collected and destroyed at once. All drinking water should be boiled before being used. General vaccination orders should be issued, as a serious epidemic of smallpox threatens Ohio."

We had to leave our cat behind. I am worried about her. Why did I think all our troubles would be over when the water went away?

March 28, 1913

Morning Dear Diary—It is a blessing to be home. The bad news is there mud all over downstairs. The good news is that our cat stayed upstairs. She

was very hungry when we got home. Thomas said he knows she ate some mice because he found their skeletons and did I want to see them? I said absolutely not!

Father gave us the smallpox vaccinations before he left this morning. He promised it wouldn't hurt, and it didn't. I must have looked a little bit scared, though. Mother said I was her good, brave girl. She said someday I would tell my children about how we survived the Great Flood of 1913.

I have a better idea. I will let them read about it in my diary.

The flood of 1913 was the worst Columbus has ever experienced. The water that overran the banks of the Scioto River washed away four bridges. Flood water stood 22 feet high in some parts of the city. Thousands of people lost their homes. The flood hit nearly every river city in Ohio and Indiana. One newspaper article at the time described Ohio as "a vast inland lake." Another reporter wrote, "A great mountain of water has been hurled from the clouds upon Ohio . . . Put this enormous mass of water in another form and it would fill a gigantic standpipe a mile in diameter and about five miles high."

The flood water soon drained away or seeped into the earth. People got busy cleaning up the mud and rebuilding their homes. City workers erected new flood walls to hold back the Scioto River. They also put in four bridges to replace those that had been destroyed.

It took years for the city to dry out, clean up, and rebuild after the Great Flood.

Hilliard City School District
J.W. Reason Elementary School
4790 Cemetery Road
Hilliard, Ohio 43026